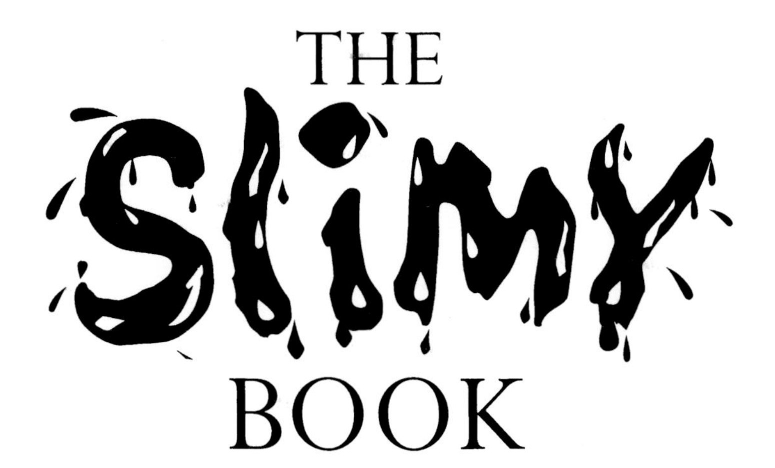
THE
Slimy
BOOK

D1419738

0 0 SEP 2016

30131 03834692 7
LONDON BOROUGH OF BARNET

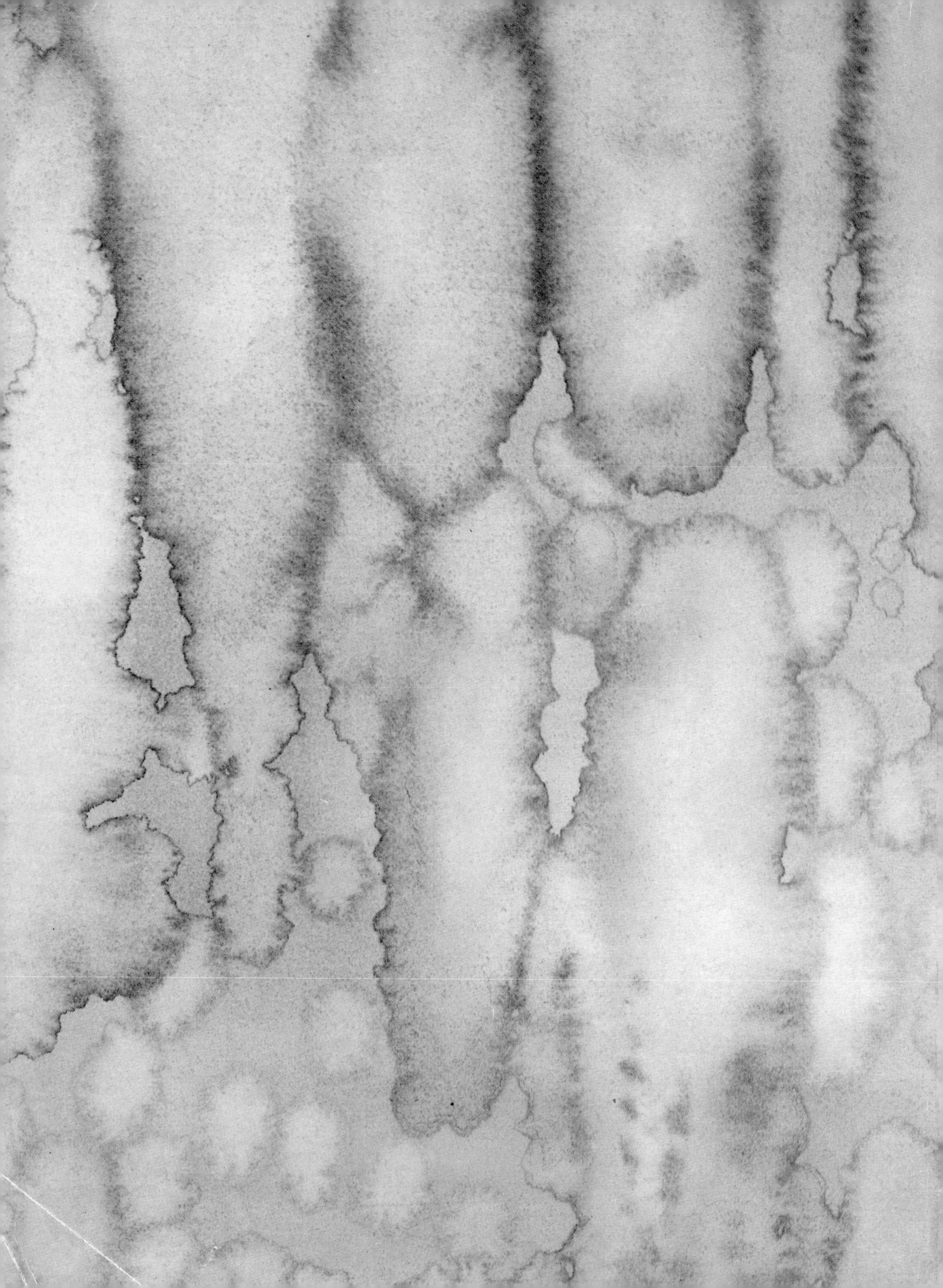

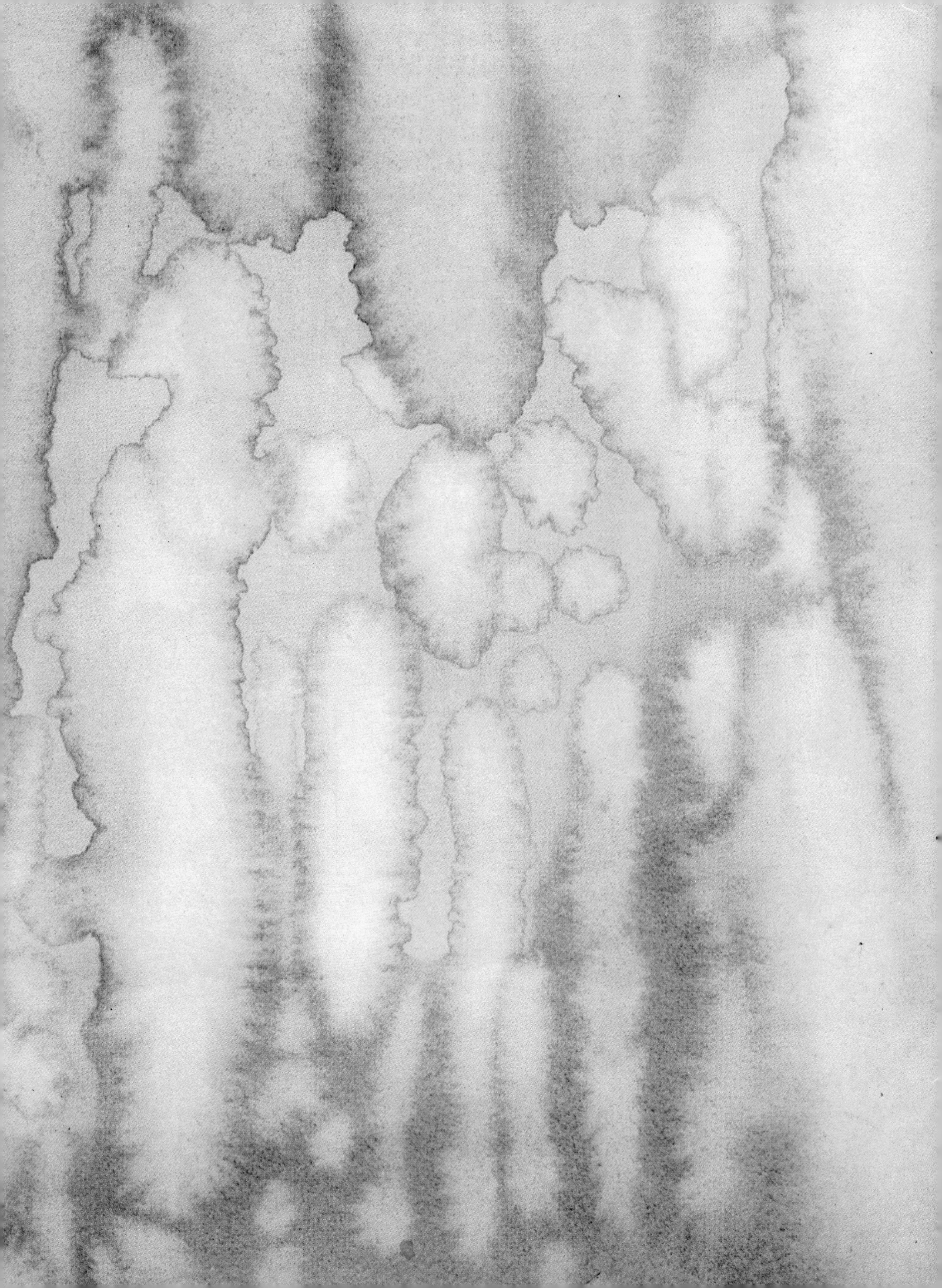

Other books by Babette Cole

Animals Scare Me Stiff
Dr Dog
Drop Dead
Hair in Funny Places
Mummy Laid an Egg
The Hairy Book
The Silly Book
The Smelly Book
Truelove
Two of Everything

0 0 SEP 2016

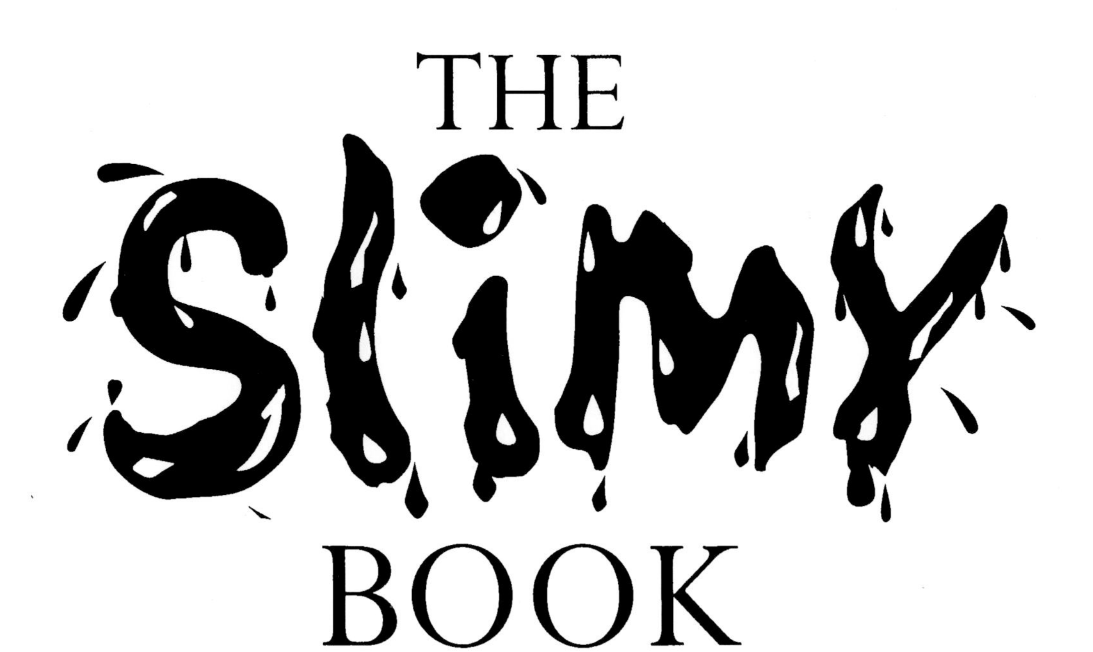

Babette Cole

RED FOX

Sticky, sludgy, slippy slime,

the sloppy, ploppy, creepy kind.

Slime in
my pocket,

in my shoe.

Is it
custard?

Is it glue?

Hello, slimy squids,

slugs,

snails,

and
slippery
toads
in slimy
pails.

Slimy worms on the lawn,

newts
from
ponds,

and green
frog-spawn.

Octopi with slimy limbs
eat little fish with slimy fins!

Fat ladies rub slime on their skin,

hoping it will make them thin!

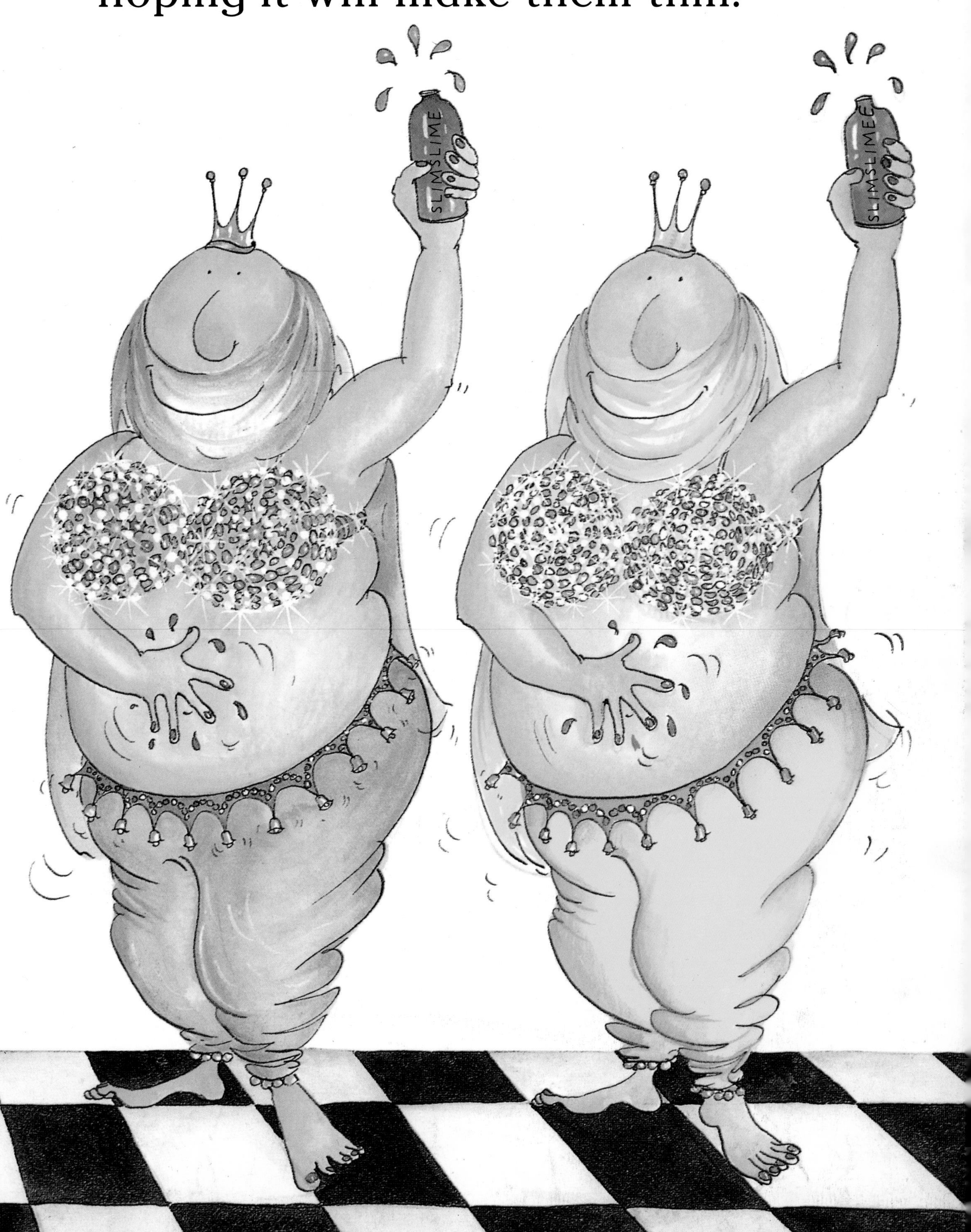

People with no teeth, it's said,
can't eat a slimy pickled egg!

Slime loves dribbling down the drain,
and blocking all the pipes again!

Maybe it's lurking in the loo.
Careful! It could pounce on you!

I wonder how it really feels,
slurping slimy
jellied eels . . .

Here's someone having slime for tea,
I hope they never invite me!

CLOCK
WS
TABLE SLIME
Cup-a-Slime

Blimey! Slimy,
oodles noodles,
slimy sausages
for poodles . . .

Slimy butter,
slimy jelly,

slimy baked beans,

bulging belly!

I should have listened
to my Mum,

who said, "Don't chew
that bubblegum!
It is the slimy
kind that clings . . .

to your nose and other things!"

And I wish
I hadn't tried
those horrid sweets
with slime inside!

With all the slime inside this book,
strange creatures came to have a look,

slimy green things straight from Mars,
and planets far beyond the stars,

they ate it up and left behind
trails of yellow
glistening slime!

Goodbye, you slimy things
I've seen . . .

I'm glad that you
were all a dream!

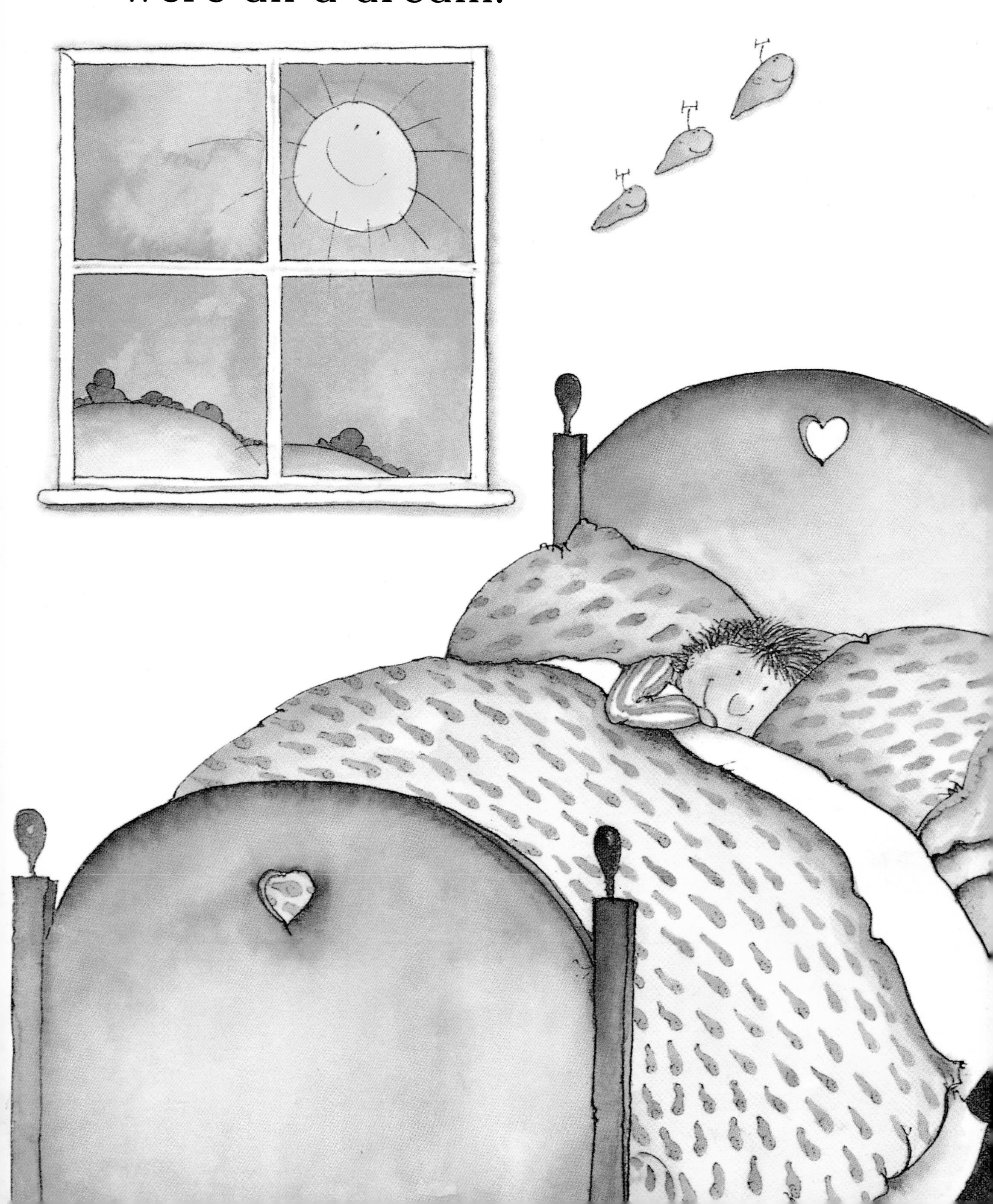

THE SLIMY BOOK
A RED FOX BOOK 0 09 943426 1

First published in Great Britain by Jonathan Cape,
an imprint of Random House Children's Books

Jonathan Cape edition published 1985
Red Fox edition published 2003

1 3 5 7 9 10 8 6 4 2

Red Fox Books are published by Random House Children's Books,
61–63 Uxbridge Road, London W5 5SA,
a division of The Random House Group Ltd,
in Australia by Random House Australia (Pty) Ltd,
20 Alfred Street, Milsons Point, Sydney, NSW 2061, Australia,
in New Zealand by Random House New Zealand Ltd,
18 Poland Road, Glenfield, Auckland 10, New Zealand,
and in South Africa by Random House (Pty) Ltd,
Endulini, 5A Jubilee Road, Parktown 2193, South Africa

THE RANDOM HOUSE GROUP Limited Reg. No. 954009
www.**kids**at**randomhouse**.co.uk

A CIP catalogue record for this book is available from the British Library.

Printed in Hong Kong

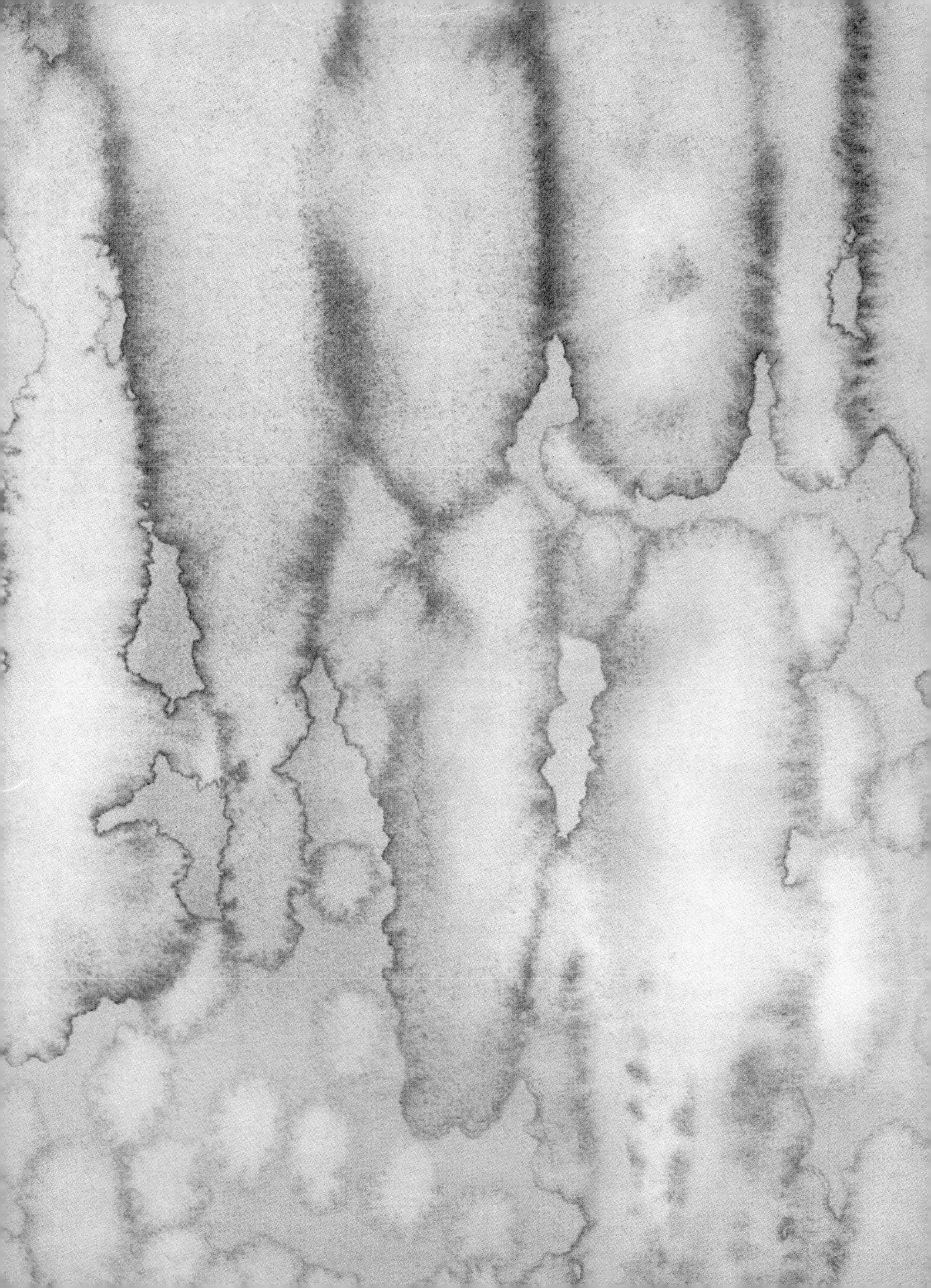

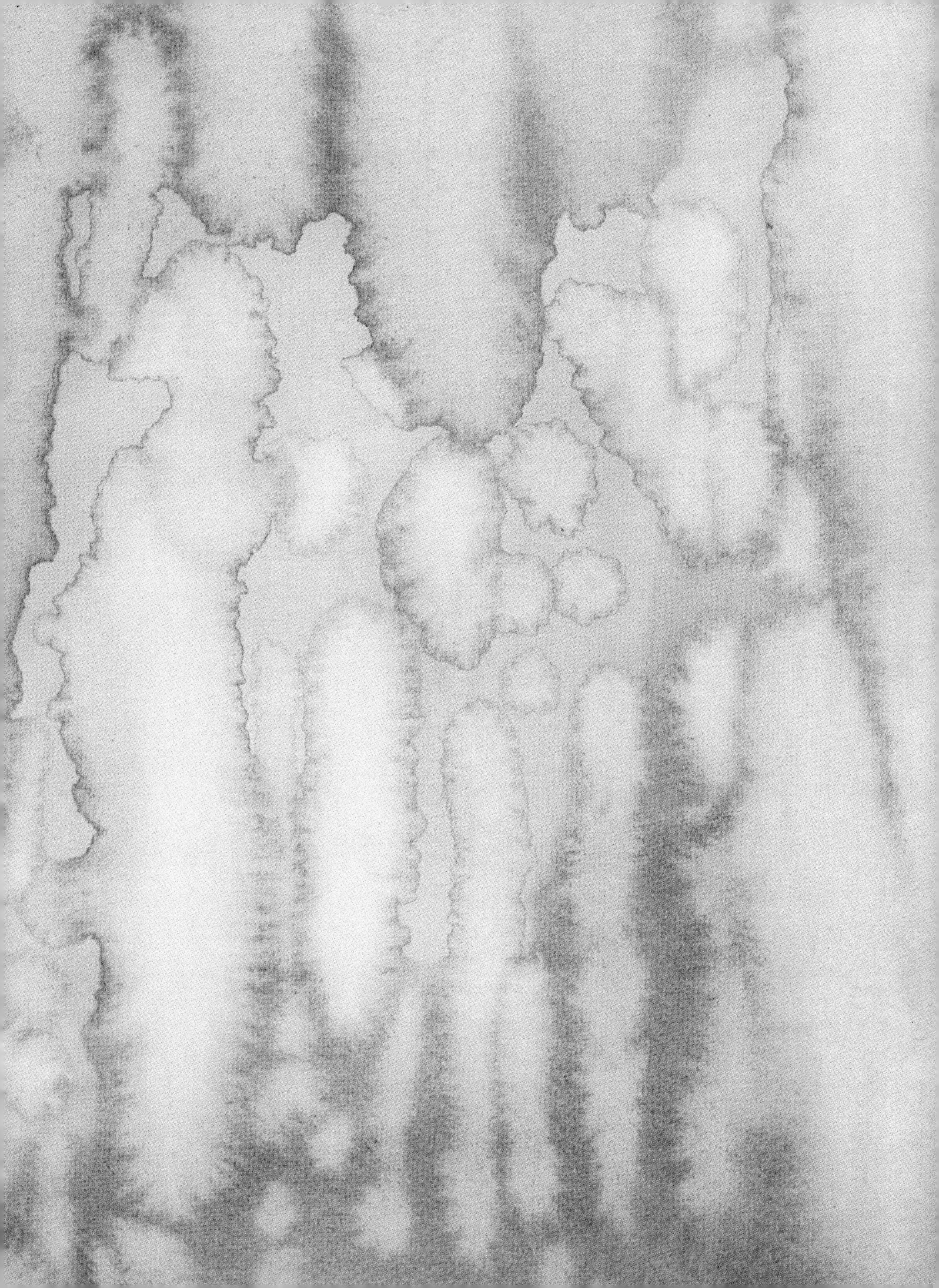

More Red Fox picture books for you to enjoy

ELMER
by David McKee 0099697203

MUMMY LAID AN EGG!
by Babette Cole 0099299119

THE RUNAWAY TRAIN
by Benedict Blathwayt 0099385716

DOGGER
by Shirley Hughes 009992790X

WHERE THE WILD THINGS ARE
by Maurice Sendak 0099408392

OLD BEAR
by Jane Hissey 0099265761

ALFIE GETS IN FIRST
by Shirley Hughes 0099855607

OI! GET OFF OUR TRAIN
by John Burningham 009985340X

GORGEOUS!
by Caroline Castle and Sam Childs 0099400766